Miss Suki Is Kooky!

Miss Suki Is Kooky!

Dan Gutman

Pictures by
Jim Paillot

HarperTrophy®
An Imprint of HarperCollins Publishers

Miss Suki Is Kooky!

Text copyright © 2007 by Dan Gutman

Illustrations copyright © 2007 by Jim Paillot

Library of Congress Cataloging-in-Publication Data is available.

ISBN-10: 0-06-123474-5 (lib. bdg.) — ISBN-13: 978-0-06-123474-3 (lib. bdg.)

ISBN-10: 0-06-123473-7 (pbk.) — ISBN-13: 978-0-06-123473-6 (pbk.)

Typography by Joel Tippie

❖

First Harper Trophy edition, 2007

19 20 BRR 40 39 38 37 36 35 34

To Emma

Contents

The Weirdest Thing in the History of the World

My name is A.J. and I hate school.

It was Monday morning, and all the girls were playing with these fake makeup kits that they got at some birthday party over the weekend. I thought I was gonna throw up.

"Picture Day is in three weeks," said my teacher, Miss Daisy, as she handed us each a piece of paper. "A photographer is going to come and take pictures of every student in school. So make sure your parents fill out this form if they want to order pictures."

"I *love* getting my picture taken!" said this annoying girl with curly brown hair named Andrea Young. (The girl's name is Andrea Young, that is. Not her hair. Hair doesn't have a name.)

"Me too," said this crybaby girl named Emily, who always agrees with anything Andrea says.

"They should take your pictures," I

suggested, "and burn them."

My friends Ryan and Michael laughed. Emily looked like she was going to cry.

"It just so happens that Emily and I are very photogenic," Andrea told us.

"Wow!" I said. "You can read minds?"

"'Photogenic' means you look good in pictures, dumbhead."

"That's good," I said, "because you're ugly in real life."

"Oh, snap!" said Michael.

"Do you know where they should put your picture, Arlo?" asked Andrea.

"Where?" I asked. I hate when she calls me by my real name.

"In the post office," she said, "with all

3

those pictures of criminals and bank rob-bers and murderers."

"Oh, snap!" said Ryan.

"So is your face," I told Andrea. Any time somebody says something mean to you, always say, "So is your face." Even if it doesn't make any sense. That's the first rule of being a kid.

"Enough chitchat," said Miss Daisy. "We have library now with Mrs. Roopy."

"Yay!" said all the girls.

"Boo!" said all the boys.

Bummer in the summer! Libraries are boring. Do you know why? Because they're filled with books! And there's nothing more boring than a book. Why are you even reading this one?

Library would be even more boring if we didn't have a librarian like Mrs. Roopy. She's always dressed up like somebody else, whether it's Little Bo Peep or Johnny Appleseed. Mrs. Roopy is loopy.

When we got to the library, we saw Mrs. Roopy dressed up like a giant bird, with lots of feathers and a beak.

"Why are you dressed up like a bird, Mrs. Roopy?" asked Neil, who we call the nude kid even though he wears clothes.

"Squawk! Squawk! Squawk!" shouted Mrs. Roopy as she flapped her wings. "Who's Roopy? My name is Rappy. I'm a peregrine falcon, the main character in *The Fearless Falcon*.* It's a wonderful book written and illustrated by the famous children's book author Miss Suki Kabuki."

Mrs. Roopy read us a few chapters of the book. It's about this falcon that sees its reflection in a window and thinks it's an enemy. So it attacks its own reflection

---

*If you ever see one of these things in a book, it means you're supposed to look down.

by flying right into the glass. *Bam!*

Man, was that bird dumb.**

"That's the saddest story I ever heard!" Emily said, with tears in her eyes. That girl will cry over any old thing.

After library we went to the art room. Ms. Hannah, our art teacher, was waiting for us.

"Today we're going to draw pictures of Rappy, the peregrine falcon in *The Fearless Falcon*," said Ms. Hannah. "It was written and illustrated by the famous children's book author Miss Suki Kabuki."

Hmm, that was strange. Why were we

**Ha-ha-ha! Made you look down! Man, you'll fall for anything!

7

doing something with the *same* book in both library *and* art?

After we finished drawing our pictures and cleaning up the art room, it was time to go to music with Mr. Loring.

"Today we're going to sing a song about a falcon named Rappy," said Mr. Loring. "He's the main character in *The Fearless Falcon*, which was written and illustrated by Miss Suki Kabuki."

This was getting really weird!

After music class was over, we went to the computer lab.

"Good morning," said Mrs. Yonkers, our computer teacher. "Today we're going to visit www.sukikabuki.com. That's the

website of children's
book author Miss
Suki Kabuki."

What the heck
was going on?!
How come *all*
the teachers were
talking about this dumb children's book
author? It was the weirdest thing in the
history of the world.

After we finished computer lab, we
went back to our class to get ready for
lunch. Suddenly I heard a knock at the
door. Miss Daisy answered it.

It was Mr. Klutz, the principal! He has
no hair at all.

"I have big news!" Mr. Klutz announced. "Guess who will be coming to visit our school in three weeks?"

"Who?" we all asked.

"A famous children's book author," Mr. Klutz said. "Her name is Miss Suki Kabuki!"

Children's Books Are Dumb

So *that*'s why all the teachers were talking about Miss Suki Kabuki. She was coming to visit our school. I never met a real live author before. Come to think of it, I never met any dead ones either.

"Wow!" said all the girls.

"Who cares?" said all the boys.

Mr. Klutz was so excited about the author visit, he had to go tell all the other classes the news.

"I *love* Miss Suki Kabuki!" said Andrea, who loves books and anything else that's boring. "She's my favorite author!"

"Never heard of her before today," I said.

"Well, maybe if you picked up a book once in a while, Arlo, then you would know who she is."

"Hey, I picked up a book once," I said. "And then I put it back down again."

Andrea had to show everybody how smart she was by naming some of Miss Suki Kabuki's books, like *The Fearless*

Falcon, *The Reluctant Rhino*, and *The Courageous Crane*.

"That's right, Andrea," said Miss Daisy. "Suki Kabuki has written a lot of great books. She's coming all the way to America from Japan because she won the Blueberry Award. That's an award that is given for the best children's book of the year. Miss Suki is only visiting a few schools in America, and ours is one of them! We're very lucky our PTA was able to get her."

"I knew Miss Suki was coming," said Andrea, who loves telling people how much she knows.

"How did you know?" asked Neil the nude kid.

"My mother is vice president of the PTA," Andrea said. "She knows everything."

"I'm sure it was very hard to get Miss Suki to come and visit us," Miss Daisy said. "She lives in the rainforest, where she writes all about those animals."

"I love animals," Andrea said. "When I grow up, I want to be a veterinarian."

"You're not going to eat meat?" I asked.

"No, dumbhead," said Andrea. "That's a *vegetarian*. A veterinarian is an animal doctor."

"It is not," I said.

"It is too," Andrea said.

We went back and forth like that for a while. And then I came up with a genius idea to win the argument.

"Oh, yeah?" I said. "Well, a veterinarian who doesn't eat meat is a vegetarian. So nah-nah-nah boo-boo!"

In her face! No wonder they put me in the gifted and talented program.

"I can't believe Miss Suki is coming to our school," said Emily, all excited. "Do you think she'll sign autographs?"

"I don't know," said Miss Daisy, who doesn't know anything. "Maybe she will if you kids are on your best behavior."

I didn't want Miss Suki's autograph. I had never even heard of her or any of her dumb books before. How come we have to have an author visit anyway? Why can't we have a professional skateboarder instead? That would be cool.

Children's books are dumb, if you ask me. So anybody who writes children's books must be dumb, too. Except for Dr. Seuss, of course. The only books I read are by Dr. Seuss. He was cool, even if he wasn't a real doctor.

"Why can't we invite Dr. Seuss to our school?" I asked.

"Because he's dead, dumbhead," said Andrea.

"So is your face," I replied.

I Hate Andrea and She Hates Me

"Miss Daisy, please come to the office," Mr. Klutz said over the loudspeaker a few days later. "Oh, by the way, Picture Day and Author Day are both going to be two weeks from Friday. So we will be killing two birds with one stone, you might say. Thank you for your attention."

"Killing birds is mean!" said Emily.

"It's just an expression, dumbhead," I told her. "Killing two birds with one stone means doing two things at once."

"I knew that," Emily lied. She looked like she was going to cry, as usual.

Miss Daisy was still in the office. Andrea and Emily pulled those fake makeup kits out of their desks again. They were looking in these little round mirrors and fussing with their hair.

"You look fabulous, Emily," said Andrea.

"No, *you* look fabulous, Andrea," said Emily.

"What do you think I should wear for Picture Day?" asked Andrea. "My blue skirt or the red one with the boat on it?"

"Oh, definitely the blue one," Emily said. "It brings out your eyes."

"I think I need more lipstick," said Andrea.

"I need to moisturize," said Emily.

"Ugh," I said. "What is your problem?" I thought I was gonna throw up.

"We're making ourselves pretty," Andrea told me.

"That's good," I replied, "because you couldn't make yourselves any uglier."

"You're mean!" said Emily.

"Why don't you just put paper bags over your heads so we don't have to look at you?" I suggested.

"Very funny, Arlo," said Andrea. "When

I'm a teenager, I'm going to put on *real* makeup, and I'll be even more beautiful. Then you'll ask me out on a date, and I'll say I'm busy because I don't want to hurt your feel- ings by telling you that I don't like you."

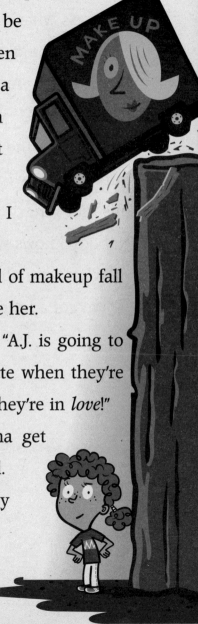

Why can't a truck full of makeup fall on Andrea's head? I hate her.

"Oooooh!" said Ryan. "A.J. is going to ask Andrea out on a date when they're teenagers. That means they're in *love*!"

"When are you gonna get married?" asked Michael.

Just then, Miss Daisy

rushed back from the office.

"Guess what?" she said.

I was going to answer by shouting "Your butt!" Any time somebody says "Guess what," you have to say "Your butt." That's the first rule of being a kid. But Miss Daisy is a grown-up, and grown-ups get angry when you say "butt." Nobody knows why.

"What?" we all shouted.

"We got a letter from Miss Suki!"

Here Comes the Big-Shot Author

Miss Daisy read the letter we got from Miss Suki:

To my dear friends at
Ella Mentry School,
I can't wait to meet you!
I love children and look forward

to visiting your school. I will
have a big surprise to show
you. See you soon!
Sayonara,
Miss Suki Kabuki

Miss Daisy tacked the letter up on the
bulletin board. She was so excited that a
real live, famous author actually took the
time to write to us. She made us write
letters back to Miss Suki, draw pictures
for her, and think of questions to ask her
when she arrived.

For the next two weeks, pretty much all
we did at school was get ready for Miss
Suki's visit. Mrs. Patty, the secretary, put

up a big chart in the office that said
COUNTDOWN TO PICTURE DAY AND AUTHOR
DAY. Every day, she crossed off a number
so everybody would know how many
days were left.

14 . . . 13 . . . 12 . . . 11 . . .

The reading specialist, Mr. Macky,
came into our class and told us all about
Miss Suki's books. Man, that lady sure
likes animals! I think she likes animals
better than people. That's why she lives
in the rainforest instead of in a regular
house with her family. People who live
with animals are weird. I wondered if
Miss Suki runs around the rainforest in a
loincloth like Tarzan.

10 . . . 9 . . . 8 . . . 7 . . .

In science, Mr. Docker taught us all about peregrine falcons, because that's what Miss Suki wrote about in *The Fearless Falcon*. Peregrine falcons are called raptors, and they eat other birds, like pigeons and ducks. Yuck! Mr. Docker said they don't have teeth, so they use their beak and their razor-sharp toenails called talons to tear into flesh. Ouch! Their eyesight is so sharp that they can spot a rabbit from a mile away. *And* they're the fastest birds in the world. They can fly almost two hundred miles an hour. One time my dad drove eighty miles an hour, and a policeman pulled

him over and gave him a ticket. But I
don't think peregrine falcons have to
obey the speed limit.

6...5...4...3...

Some classes made shoe-box scenes
from Miss Suki's books. Some classes
made sculptures of Miss Suki's animal
friends out of Popsicle sticks. Our class
made a "Welcome" sign in art with Ms.
Hannah. We also
made a long red
carpet out of con-
struction paper

so Miss Suki could make a grand entrance into school. We also made acrostics out of Miss Suki's name, like this:

Marvelous!
Interesting!
Serious!
Same as the last S!

See above!
Understanding!
Knowledgeable!
I can't wait to meet her!

Finally, all that was left on the COUNT-DOWN TO PICTURE DAY AND AUTHOR DAY chart was a big number 1. It was the day before Miss Suki would arrive. Everybody was excited, except for me. You would have thought the president or the pope or Tony Hawk was coming to our school.

In the vomitorium that day, the lunch lady, Ms. LaGrange, prepared a traditional Japanese dish called chicken teriyaki in honor of Miss Suki. It's chicken with teriyaki sauce poured over it, so it has the perfect name.

I sat with Ryan and Michael and Neil the nude kid. Ryan was opening peanut shells by cracking them on his head. Michael blew air into his lunch bag and popped it to freak out the girls. Neil the nude kid put crackers in his eye sockets.

Andrea and Emily and their annoying girly friends were at the next table talking about girly things again.

"Should I put my hair in a ponytail for Picture Day?" asked Andrea. "Or should I wear a bow?"

"A ponytail, of course!" replied Emily.

Ugh! I thought I was gonna throw up.

"I bet Miss Suki is going to come in a

limousine," said Michael.

"Maybe she'll come in a helicopter," said Ryan.

"She lives in the rainforest," I said. "Maybe she will swing in on a vine like Tarzan. That would be cool."

"What do you think the big surprise is that she talked about in her letter?" asked Neil the nude kid.

"Beats me," we all said.

Lunch was almost over, so we all had to scrape the food off our trays into the big garbage can.

"I hope Miss Suki will sign my autograph book tomorrow," Emily told the girls. "I took it to Disney World and got it signed by Mickey and Goofy."

"Those are just teenagers dressed up like Mickey and Goofy, dumbhead," I told her.

"They are not!" Emily whined. "They're the *real* Mickey and Goofy!" Emily would have cried, but we had to go back to class, so I guess she didn't have time.

When we got to Miss Daisy's room, guess who walked into the door? Nobody! If you walked into a door, it would hurt. But guess who walked into the door*way*?

It was Mr. Klutz and Mrs. Roopy!

"Are you excited about Picture Day tomorrow?" asked Mr. Klutz.

"Are you excited about Author Day tomorrow?" asked Mrs. Roopy.

"Yes!" yelled all the girls.

"No!" yelled all the boys.

"I can't *wait* to meet Miss Suki," Mr. Klutz said, "because I love animals too. In my younger days, I used to work over the summer in a zoo."

"Wow!" we all said, even though Mr. Klutz didn't say anything that interesting. When grown-ups tell you boring stuff

about their younger days, you should always pretend to be interested. That's the first rule of being a kid.

"Remember," Mr. Klutz continued, "Miss Suki is our guest. I'm sure you'll be on your best behavior and treat her with respect. We want to show Miss Suki what kind of wonderful students we have at Ella Mentry School. By the way, I invited Dr. Carbles, the president of the Board of Education, too. Isn't that exciting?"

"Yes!" we all said, even though it totally wasn't.

After Mr. Klutz was finished talking, Mrs. Roopy said she had a few words to say.

"Miss Suki will probably give you the chance to ask questions," Mrs. Roopy told us. "Remember, a question is *not* a story about yourself. A question is when you *ask* somebody something. And whatever you do, don't ask Miss Suki personal questions like how old she is or how much money she makes."

We all promised to be good listeners and not to ask any stupid questions.

Well, after three weeks of getting ready, it was almost time for the big day. To tell you the truth, I was getting sick of Miss Suki, and she hadn't even shown up yet.

Miss Suki
Finally Arrives

When we got to school the next morning, there was a big sign on the front lawn:

ELLA MENTRY SCHOOL WELCOMES

MISS SUKI KABUKI

FOR AUTHOR DAY AND PICTURE DAY!

All the girls were dressed up for Picture Day. All the boys were dressed like slobs, as usual.

After we put our backpacks in our cubbies, Andrea and Emily took out their little mirrors and tried to make themselves look pretty. That would make a good movie—*Mission Impossible*!

Miss Daisy told us that our pictures would be taken at the end of the day, after the author visit. Because there was so much going on at school, we would have to miss math. Yeah, baby! I *hate* math.

Everybody was whispering, "Where's Miss Suki?" "Is Miss Suki here yet?" We pressed our faces against the window so we could be the first to see Miss Suki when she arrived.

And then I saw her! I was looking

through the window between our class-room and the hallway when a lady walked by on the red construction paper carpet that was taped to the floor. I recognized her face from the author photo in her book. Miss Suki was pulling a rolling cart with a big box on it. She was a skinny little lady, not much bigger than a kid. It looked like a gust of wind could knock her over.

"It's her!" I shouted. "Miss Suki is here!"

Everybody made a mad dash into the hallway. That's when the most amazing thing in the history of the world happened. The wheel of Miss Suki's rolling cart got caught on the red carpet or something and it made her trip. She fell flat on her face.

We all ran over to help her.

"Why is that paper all over the floor?" Miss Suki asked.

"It's not paper," Ryan told her. "It's a red carpet, so you could make a grand entrance."

"Can you please get rid of it?" she said. "I've had a hard day already. My plane was delayed, and the taxi driver got lost on the way over here."

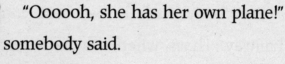

"Ooooooh, she has her own plane!" somebody said.

"Oooooh, she has her own taxi!" somebody else said.

"Are you *really* the famous children's book author Miss Suki Kabuki?" I asked.

"Yes, I am!" she replied, and she shook my hand.

"Oooooh, I touched somebody famous!" I said. "I'm never going to wash this hand again!"

"Big deal, Arlo," said Andrea. "You probably never wash your hands anyway."

"Oh, snap!" said Ryan.

"So is your face," I told Andrea.

"What's in the box, Miss Suki?" asked Emily.

"Oh, you'll find out later," she said. "It's

41

my *mystery* box. But first, can you tell me where the office is? I need to introduce myself to your principal, Mr. Putz."

"It's *Klutz*!" everybody shouted, and we told Miss Suki how to get to the office.

We were so excited that we were the first class in school to meet Miss Suki. The bad part was, we had to wait a million hundred hours for her assembly to start. First, she had to visit the kindergarten trolls. After that she had to talk to the fifth and sixth graders. Then she had to have lunch with the teachers. *Then* she had to sign all the books that kids ordered.

Finally it was time for our assembly. Andrea and Emily wanted to bring their dumb mirrors along, but Miss Daisy said they couldn't. Nah-nah-nah boo-boo on them.

We walked a million hundred miles to the all-purpose room. But even *I* was a little excited by then, so it didn't seem that far.

When we finally arrived, we saw an easel on the stage, and Miss Suki's mystery box.

I wanted to sit with my friends, but Miss Daisy made me sit between Andrea and Emily.

"Boy, girl, boy, girl," Miss Daisy said. "Crisscross applesauce." (That's grown-up talk for "Sit down and cross your legs.")

When everybody was seated, Mrs.

Roopy made a peace sign with her fingers, which means "Shut up." She was wearing her bird suit again and held a big slab of wood under her wing. It looked like one of those boards my mom uses in the kitchen when she chops up food.

"Is everybody excited?" Mrs. Roopy asked.

"Yes!" the girls and even the boys shouted.

"Look what I've got!" Mrs. Roopy said, holding up the slab of wood so we could see. It had shiny metal on the front with the words BLUE- BERRY AWARD on it.

"This is what Miss Suki Kabuki won for *The Fearless Falcon*!" said Mrs. Roopy. "She just got it yesterday. I can't believe she said I could hold it! Isn't that cool?"

"Wow!" we all said, even though it wasn't that cool.

"Well, you kids haven't been waiting three weeks to listen to *me* talk," Mrs. Roopy said. "So, I'm proud to finally introduce Ella Mentry School's favorite author, Miss Suki Kabuki!"

Miss Suki Is a Big Crybaby

Everybody clapped and cheered when Miss Suki came out on stage. Then we all got quiet so we could hear what she had to say.

"Hello! Thank you so much for inviting me to your—"

At that very second, the strangest thing

in the history of the world happened. All these bells started clanging so loud that we had to cover our ears. Miss Suki freaked out.

"FIRE!" she shouted. "The school is on fire! Run for your lives!" And then she went running out of the room, hugging her mystery box.

Miss Suki is kooky!

It wasn't a fire. It was just a fire *drill*. Any dumbhead knows that once in a while the bells ring and we all have to go stand out in the playground.

"Line up in single file," Miss Daisy told us.

We marched out of the school. When

we got to the playground, Mr. Klutz was running around trying to catch up with Miss Suki. All the girls were complaining that the wind was messing up their hair and it wouldn't look good for Picture Day.

"That would be cool if the school really *did* burn down," I told Ryan and Michael.

"Yeah," Ryan agreed. "Then we could toast marshmallows."

Miss Suki was standing near our class, still hugging her mystery box, when Mr. Klutz finally caught up with her.

"Maybe this just isn't my day," Miss Suki said, shaking her head.

"Oh, don't worry," Mr. Klutz told her. "The fire drill wasn't supposed to happen today. Nothing else could possibly go wrong."

The bell rang again, which meant the fire drill was over. We went back inside to the all-purpose room, and Mrs. Roopy introduced Miss Suki all over again.

"Well, *that* was exciting," said Miss Suki. "Thanks for inviting me to your school. I love books and reading. Don't you?"

"Yes!" said all the girls.

"No!" said all the boys.

"Books can take you to different worlds," said Miss Suki.

"So can spaceships," somebody yelled.

"What's in that box, Miss Suki?" somebody else yelled. Mrs. Roopy jumped up

and grabbed the microphone.

"Please don't call out any questions yet," Mrs. Roopy said. "Miss Suki will answer your questions at the end of her talk." She handed the microphone back to Miss Suki.

"When I was a little girl growing up in Japan," Miss Suki said, "my mother took me to the library every week. And by the time I was ten years old, I had read every book in that library. That's when I knew I was going to grow up and become a children's book author."

"Wow," we all said, even though it wasn't that interesting.

"Ever since I was little, I loved animals," Miss Suki told us. "That's why I write about them and draw pictures of them."

Miss Suki drew a picture of a bird on the easel. Well, she didn't really draw a picture of a *bird on an easel*. She drew a picture of a bird on a tree, and the *picture* was on the easel. Anyway, she drew really fast. Miss Suki is a good drawer.***

"This is Rappy," she said as she finished the picture. "He is a raptor, and the main character of my book *The Fearless Falcon*."

Then Mrs. Roopy dimmed the lights, and Miss Suki turned on this machine that shows pictures on a big screen. We saw pictures of Miss Suki in the rainforest with all kinds of animals like monkeys and weird birds and stuff. It was cool.

"May I read you a chapter from *The*

***But she was not the same kind of drawer you put stuff in. That would be weird.

Fearless Falcon?" asked Miss Suki.

"Yes!" we all shouted.

Miss Suki read us the part where Rappy sees his reflection in a window and thinks it's another raptor, so he attacks himself and crashes into the glass. He nearly dies. It was really sad and exciting when Miss Suki read it.

And then something really weird happened. Miss Suki started to cry. She had to stop reading. Mrs. Roopy gave her a tissue.

"What's the matter, Miss Suki?" asked Emily.

"Remember the letter I wrote you?" Miss Suki asked, wiping her eyes. "I said I would have a big surprise to show you. Well, here it is."

She went over to her mystery box and lifted up the latch. Then she opened the door of the box. Do you know what was inside?

I'm not going to tell you.

Okay, okay, I'll tell you. But you'll have to read the next chapter. So nah-nah-nah boo-boo on you.

Rappy the Raptor Is Cool

Miss Suki opened the mystery box and took out a big bird. It let out a loud SQUAWK!

"This," she announced, "is Rappy. He's my inspiration for *The Fearless Falcon.*"

"Wow!" we all said. Now that really *was* interesting.

"I found him on the ground outside a building that was covered with windows," Miss Suki told us as the bird perched on her finger. "Rappy must have seen his reflection and rammed into the glass, trying to attack it. His parents were nowhere to be found, so I brought him home with me. Poor Rappy nearly died. That's what gave me the idea for my book." Miss Suki started crying again.

I turned around. Some of the kids looked like they were gonna cry too. Sheesh, get a grip! I mean, the bird was still alive.

Rappy showed off his feathers. He must have been four feet from wing to wing.

"Squawk! Squawk!" squawked Rappy.

"He's intimidating!" whispered Andrea, who likes to show off by saying big words.

"And scary!" whispered Emily.

"They had raptors in that movie *Jurassic Park*," I whispered to the girls. "One of them ripped some guy's head off while he was sitting on a toilet bowl."

"Stop trying to scare Emily," whispered Andrea.

"Rappy is my baby," Miss Suki said, and she gave Rappy a kiss on his beak. "Isn't he beautiful?"****

People who kiss birds are weird.

Miss Suki told us that Rappy's talons

****Boys can't be beautiful. Boys can be *handsome*. *Girls* are beautiful. Especially girls like Mrs. Cooney, our school nurse. But not girls like Andrea.

are four inches long and as sharp as carv-
ing knives.

"If he wanted to, he could kill a lion,"
said Miss Suki.

"Wow!" Michael shouted. "Did you
bring a lion, too?"

"Yeah," Ryan said, "we want to see
Rappy kill it!"

"Oh, Rappy is harmless," Miss Suki told
us. "He wouldn't hurt a fly."

I wasn't worried about Rappy hurting
flies. I was worried about Rappy flying away
from Miss Suki's hand and using those
talons to rip my head off.

"I'm sure he wouldn't hurt any of our
students," said Mrs. Roopy.

"Until recently, peregrine falcons were

an endangered species," Miss Suki told us. "Does anybody know what 'endangered' means?"

Andrea's hand shot up in the air, of course. Any time anybody asks anything, Andrea's hand is always the first one to go up.

"'Endangered' means there aren't many of them left," Andrea said when she got called on. She was all proud of herself. Big deal. Any dumbhead knows what "endangered" means.

"That's right," said Miss Suki. "Peregrine falcons almost became extinct in the 1960s. Does anybody know what 'extinct' means?"

HA-HA-HA-HA-HA-HA-HA

Andrea put her hand in the air, but I guess Miss Suki didn't want to call on her twice in a row. So I put my hand up, and she called on me instead.

"'Extinct' is when something smells really bad," I said. "Like, 'Whew, that extincts!'"

Everybody laughed, even though I

didn't say anything funny.

"Good answer, dumbhead," Andrea whispered.

"Actually," Miss Suki said, "a species is extinct when there are none of them left. So I must be *very* careful with Rappy."

Rappy squawked like crazy when Miss Suki put him back in his box. Then she thanked us for listening to her talk. All in all, I'd say her talk was almost not boring.

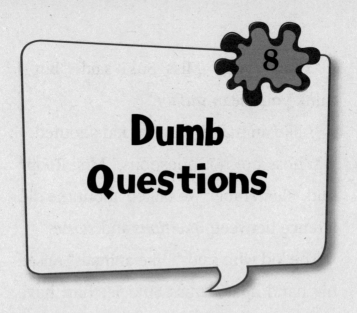

Dumb Questions

We all clapped and cheered again for Miss Suki. You're supposed to clap at the end of an assembly because you're so happy that it's over.

"That was wonderful," said Mrs. Roopy. "Does anybody have any questions?"

"You're a great arthur!" some kid yelled.

"Thank you!" Miss Suki said. "But I think you mean *author*."

"I like animals!" another kid shouted.

"Those are not questions," Mrs. Roopy said. "Remember, we talked about the difference between *questions* and *stories*."

The kid who said "I like animals" raised his hand again. Miss Suki let him have another chance to ask a question.

"Did you know that I like animals?" the kid asked.

"I didn't know that," said Miss Suki.

"Can I have your autograph?" some other kid yelled.

"Actually, I just signed four hundred books in the library," Miss Suki said. "I'm pretty tired."

"All right!" I said. "She'll sign autographs!"

"Will you sign my cast?" some kid yelled.

"Will you sign my shirt?"

"Will you sign my head?"

Mrs. Roopy jumped up and told us that Miss Suki only had time to answer questions, *not* sign autographs. So everyone started waving their hands in the air.

"What's your favorite color?"

"What's your favorite food?"

"What's your favorite football team?"

"What's your favorite Life Savers flavor?"

"What's your favorite reality TV show?"

It looked like Miss Suki was getting tired of answering questions. But if we stopped asking questions, we'd have to go to math. So everyone kept asking questions.

"Will you write a book about *us*?"

"Did you come here in a limousine?"

"Can I go to the bathroom?"

"When do we get our pictures taken?"

"How much money do you make?"

"How old are you?"

Mrs. Roopy slapped herself on the forehead.

"How old do you *think* I am?" asked Miss Suki, putting her hands on her hips.

"Eighty?" someone guessed.

Miss Suki looked mad. Mrs. Roopy jumped up to tell us there was no more time for questions.

"I'm *forty*!" Miss Suki said as we were leaving the all-purpose room. She had on a mean face. I guess she didn't like our questions very much.

What's the Magic Word?

After the assembly we went back to Miss Daisy's room. It was almost time for our class to be called down to the gym to have our pictures taken. Andrea and Emily pulled out their little mirrors and started fixing their hair. It had been a full *hour* since they last fixed their hair, so they must have had a lot of hair that needed fixing.

Just then, guess who poked their heads in the door?

Nobody! Because if you poked your head in a door, it would hurt. But guess who poked their heads in the door*way*?

It was Mrs. Roopy and Miss Suki!

Mrs. Roopy was holding a stack of books and the Blueberry Award. Miss Suki was rolling Rappy's mystery box.

"We have some autographed books," Mrs. Roopy said as she handed them out. Andrea bought every one of Miss Suki's books. I didn't buy a book. Books are boring. Besides, the order form was still in

my backpack because I forgot to give it to my parents.

"Did you write any Dr. Seuss books?" I asked Miss Suki.

"I believe those were written by Dr. Seuss," she said.

"You should write some Dr. Seuss books," I suggested. "They're cool."

"I'll think about that," Miss Suki said.

"How come Dr. Seuss was allowed to call himself a doctor when he really wasn't one?" I asked her.

"You'd have to ask *him* that," replied Miss Suki.

"I can't," I told her. "He's dead."

"Do you like cheese?" asked Ryan.

"Not very much," said Miss Suki.

"Will you sign my autograph book?" asked Emily.

"Oh, okay," said Miss Suki.

"Can I have ten autographs for my cousins?" Michael asked.

Miss Suki didn't look all that happy, but she started signing the scraps of paper Michael handed her.

"You should write a book about penguins," I suggested. "Penguins are cool."

"What's your favorite kind of cheese?" asked Ryan.

Miss Suki was about to leave when Mr. Klutz made an announcement over the loudspeaker.

"Miss Daisy's class, please report to the gym to have your pictures taken."

That's when I got the greatest idea in the history of the world.

"Will you be in our class picture, Miss Suki?" I asked.

"Please? Please? Please?" everybody begged. We said *please* about a million hundred times. If you ever want to get something from a grown-up, just say *please* over and over again. The more times you say it, the better chance they will say yes. That's the first rule of being a kid.

"Well, okay," said Miss Suki.

"YAY!"

See? It's amazing. All you have to do is say one dumb word and you can get whatever you want. What a scam!

Say Cheese!

We walked Miss Suki to the gym. Mrs. Roopy brought along the Blueberry Award.

"Miss Suki, I've read all your books," said Andrea, who never misses the chance to brownnose a grown-up, "and I have a question."

"What is it?"

"Well, in *The Reluctant Rhino*, you

wrote that Ricky the Rhino ate a fish for lunch. But I looked it up in my encyclopedia, and rhinos are vegetarians."

"They're animal doctors?" I asked.

"No, dumbhead," Andrea said. "That's a *veterinarian*. A *vegetarian* doesn't eat meat. Rhinos are vegetarians, so a rhino wouldn't eat a fish."

"It would too," I said.

"It would not," Andrea said.

We went back and forth like that for a while. Then I came up with a genius idea to win the argument.

"A rhino that went to medical school could be a veterinarian," I said. "And veterinarians can eat meat. So there!"

Nah-nah-nah boo-boo on Andrea. In

her face! No wonder they put me in the gifted and talented program.

"Is that true?" Miss Suki asked. She looked all upset. "Rhinos are vegetarians? That ruins my whole story!"

Then Miss Suki started crying again. Man, what is her problem? That lady cries more than Emily.

When we got to the gym, the photographer lined us up in ABC order. The girls were frantically combing their hair and putting on bracelets and necklaces and earrings and all kinds of other girly stuff. I can't believe girls poke holes in their ears and hang gold things all over themselves like they're Christmas trees. What's

up with that?

"My mother said she would put my picture on our refrigerator," Andrea told us.

"So, does she put food on her camera?" I asked.

"Oh, snap!" said Ryan.

Me and the guys made funny faces when our pictures were taken. But the photographer got mad and made us do them over again.

Finally it was time to take a picture of the whole class. The photographer lined us up in three rows on the bleachers. I had to stand next to Emily. Miss Daisy stood in the back row on the left side, and Miss Suki stood on the right side.

"Hey, can Rappy be in the picture, too?" I asked. "That would be cool."

"Rappy's had a long day," Miss Suki replied. "I think he needs to rest."

"Please? Please? Please? Please? Please? Please? Please? Please? Please?"

"Well, okay," said Miss Suki.

I tell you, it works every time.

Miss Suki took Rappy out of the mystery

box and put him on her finger. Rappy turned his head around slowly to look at everybody. It was cool, but a little scary, too. He looked like he was searching for something—or *someone*—to eat. I'm glad we didn't have any pigeons or ducks in the gym.

"Don't worry," Miss Suki said. "Rappy wouldn't hurt a fly."

Emily pulled out her little mirror to fix her hair one last time.

"Okay," said the photographer. "Is everybody ready? Say 'cheese'!"

That's when the most amazing thing in the history of the world happened. Rappy must have seen his reflection in Emily's mirror, because the next thing we knew, he flew off Miss Suki's finger at two hundred miles an hour! And he was heading straight for Emily!

Just a Minor Problem

Emily was looking in her mirror. She didn't see Rappy flying at her.

"Watch out!" everybody screamed. But it was too late. Rappy rammed right into Emily! She fell off the bleachers! She was freaking out!

"EEEEEEEEEEEEEEEEEKKKK!" she screamed. "The raptor attacked me!"

Rappy freaked out too. He took off and went flying crazily around the gym. Everybody started screaming and covering their heads.

"The raptor is loose!" shouted Ryan.

"We need a doctor!" shouted the photographer.

"How about Dr. Seuss?" I suggested.

"Emily, go to Mrs. Cooney's office!" shouted Miss Daisy. "Now!"

Rappy was swooping around like he was out of his mind. Emily was crying, and for once I couldn't blame her. I'd cry too if some nutty raptor attacked me. She crawled out of the gym on her hands and knees so Rappy couldn't dive-bomb her.

"He's wild!" shouted Michael. "He'll use his razor-sharp talons and beak to tear into our flesh!"

"He's just frightened!" shouted Miss Suki. "Rappy wouldn't hurt a fly."

"He hurt Emily!" yelled Andrea.

"Don't provoke him!" Miss Suki yelled, even though none of us knew what that meant. (Well, maybe Andrea did.)

"Call Miss Lazar!" shouted Miss Daisy. Miss Lazar is the school custodian, and she can solve any problem. She must have been right down the hall, because about a second later she burst into the gym. She was holding a toilet bowl plunger.

"We have a wild raptor on our hands,"

Miss Daisy said.

"Do you want me to kill it?" asked Miss Lazar. She got into a batting stance like she was going to hit Rappy with the toilet bowl plunger.

"NO!" yelled Miss Suki. "He's endangered!"

"I have an idea," said Miss Lazar. "I could build a cage out of toilet bowl plungers and we could trap him inside. He'll never escape."

Miss Lazar is bizarre. She has a museum filled with toilet bowl plungers in her secret storage room down in the basement.

Mr. Klutz came running into the gym with his bald head.

"What seems to be the problem?" he asked.

"The raptor attacked Emily!" Miss Daisy said.

"Everyone calm down," said Mr. Klutz. "I'll take care of this. I know how to handle animals. In my younger days I used to work in a zoo."

"Please don't hurt Rappy," begged Miss Suki. "He's my baby!"

"Leave it to me," said Mr. Klutz. "Where is he?"

"UP THERE!" we all shouted.

Mr. Klutz looked up. When he saw Rappy flying around near the ceiling, he screamed.

"Quick!" he yelled. "Get me a towel!"

"Are you going to trap the raptor in a towel?" Miss Daisy asked, running into the locker room to get one.

"No," said Mr. Klutz. "I'm going to wrap the towel around my head so the raptor doesn't peck me."

That was smart. After all, Mr. Klutz's bald head is so shiny, Rappy might see his reflection—and attack!

Miss Daisy came running back with a towel. Mr. Klutz wrapped it around his bald head. Then our gym teacher, Miss Small, came racing in. She was carrying a catcher's mitt, chest protector, and shin guards.

"Here," she said. "Put these on!"

"Good idea!" Mr. Klutz said. After he put the stuff on, he looked like a real catcher. That is, if catchers wore towels on their heads.

"How will you get the raptor down

from the ceiling?" asked Miss Small.

"Hand me that mirror!" ordered Mr. Klutz. "I'll put it in the mitt. The raptor will see his reflection in the mirror and think it's his enemy. Then he'll fly right into the mitt, and I'll catch him."

Boy, Mr. Klutz should get the No Bell Prize for that genius idea. If he was a kid, he'd be in the gifted and talented program for sure.

Miss Small picked up Emily's mirror and gave it to Mr. Klutz.

"What if Rappy misses

the mitt?" asked Andrea. "Raptors have four-inch-long, razor-sharp talons they use to tear into flesh. He could kill a lion!"

Mr. Klutz grabbed Miss Suki's Blueberry Award and held it in front of him like a shield.

"This will protect me," he said.

At that moment, guess who ran through the door? Nobody, because running through a door would hurt. But guess who ran through the door*way*?

It was Dr. Carbles, the president of the Board of Education!

Author Visits Are Fun!

"Sorry I missed the assembly," he said. "What's going on here, Klutz? Why are you dressed up in that weird costume? Why is it that every time I visit this school, there's a disturbance?"

"No reason to be alarmed, sir," said Mr. Klutz. "Just a minor problem with a raptor."

"Raptor?!" exclaimed Dr. Carbles.

"Didn't one of them rip some guy's head off in *Jurassic Park*?"

"Be careful!" begged Miss Suki. "He's my baby!"

"You gave birth to a raptor?" asked Dr. Carbles.

Just then, Rappy came down from the ceiling and started swooping around the gym again. Everyone was ducking and screaming.

"Stand back!" shouted Mr. Klutz, as he waved the catcher's mitt around to attract Rappy's attention. "Come on, Rappy. Be a good boy. Come to Papa!"

I think Mr. Klutz was waving the catcher's mitt around a little too fast.

Because while he was waving it, Emily's mirror fell out. It hit the floor and broke into a million hundred little pieces.

"Oh, no!" everybody yelled.

Mr. Klutz looked at Miss Suki. Miss Suki looked at Miss Daisy. Miss Daisy looked at Mrs. Roopy. Mrs. Roopy looked at the photographer. Everybody was looking at everybody else.

Suddenly Rappy went really crazy and started flying even faster around the gym. Then he must have spotted the shiny letters on the Blueberry Award, because he dive-bombed straight toward Mr. Klutz!

Mr. Klutz didn't know what to say! He

didn't know what to do! He had to think
fast!

Just before Rappy would have rammed
into him, Mr. Klutz held up the Blueberry
Award.

Wham!

Rappy slammed right into it and broke it in half! Oooooh, that had to hurt! Rappy got it right on the kisser!

It was awesome. A real Kodak moment. Luckily the photographer was snapping pictures the whole time.

"Hooray for Mr. Klutz!" we all shouted.

Everybody was cheering. Well, everybody except for Miss Suki, who was on her knees, sobbing. Rappy didn't look too happy either. In fact, it looked like he might be dead. He was on the floor with his legs in the air, twitching.

"Is that what Mr. Klutz meant by killing two birds with one stone?" Ryan asked.

"He's dead!" Miss Suki cried. "You killed my baby!"

"He's not dead," Mr. Klutz assured her. "He's just . . . resting."

"Does this mean that Rappy is still endangered?" asked Michael. "Or is he extinct now?"

"I don't know," I said. "He smells fine to me."

"You're a bunch of monsters!" Miss Suki shouted as she scooped Rappy off

the floor. "This is the worst day of my life!"

Then she ran out of the gym crying. She didn't even take the shattered pieces of her Blueberry Award with her.

"Does this mean you won't be signing any more autographs?" I asked Miss Suki. But I don't think she heard me. She was long gone.

All in all, I thought Miss Suki's visit was really cool, especially when Rappy went berserk and attacked Emily. I mean, we got to meet a famous author, *and* we got to see Mr. Klutz dress up like a catcher with a towel around his head. But best of all, we got to miss math.

I was thinking about it. Miss Suki won the Blueberry Award by writing about a raptor that flew into a window and nearly died. And then the *same* raptor flew into the Blueberry Award and nearly died! I guess the moral of the story is that you should never bring a raptor to school. Or a Blueberry Award.

Maybe Miss Suki will be able to nurse Rappy back to health again. Maybe Mrs. Cooney will be able to nurse *Emily* back to health again. Maybe Miss Lazar will be able to fix the Blueberry Award. Maybe Emily and Andrea will stop looking at themselves in the mirror all the time because you never know when you might be attacked by a crazed raptor. Maybe we'll be able to talk Mr. Klutz into inviting another author to our school next year.

But it won't be easy!